SPECIAL THANKS TO Stephan Keller@pixabay.com for use of the photo

AF491429

Sickies

Christopher Ridge

Published by Christopher Ridge, 2023.

SICKIES

First edition. June 20, 2023.

ISBN: 979-8223771937

Written by Christopher Ridge.

Table of Contents

SICKIES 1

SMELL OF A BABY 14

SURF N' TURF 20

NIGHT CALL 32

JOHNNY HAS A GUN 45

SICKIES

Henry's father told him the Health Department was coming to shoot grandpa.

That's why grandpa was locked in his room. For his safety, his father said.

His father had a hard time getting grandpa in the room. They wrestled and fought. Grandpa was a good fighter even for as old as he was. He punched Henry's father in the face pretty good and gave him a black eye.

Henry's mother was crying, begging for it all to stop but grandpa kept punching his father like a madman. Finally, his mother knocked grandpa in the head with a meat tenderizer mallet and they dragged grandpa in his room.

At least until he gets better, his father said.

Once word gets out there's a sickie or sickies in the area men in black suits come and blow the sickie's or sickies brains out before they contaminate the whole area.

At first there are no signs. You don't know you're sick. Which makes you a carrier. From the way, Henry understood it, being a carrier was very bad and would get you shot on the spot.

This is how it would start.

Around a month or two later after the virus sets in, tiny red blisters show up on your hands making you itch like crazy. It's just like poison oak, only hundred times worse. The more you scratch the more it spreads. And it lasts for months. There is no calamine lotion to help it like that those times he got poison ivy from getting his ball out of what he thought were weeds and all mothers had to do was spread some lotion on it and it would go away.

Next comes the big fever. Once the fever hits you know the virus is getting close to the brain which makes you crazy.

Mother was the doctor in the family. She knew everything about all that health stuff and knew what to do. This was why she took their temperatures three times a day to make sure everything was ok.

It was grandpa they seemed worried about the most. His father was so afraid he was going to come through that door.

Henry understood that though. He didn't want the health department shooting grandpa.

Henry felt there was a much better way but there was no stopping them. They were going to do what they wanted to do.

They called themselves medical examiners but to Henry, they were killers. They were lying, just like his father said. This whole thing was a lie.

The whole virus thing.

Henry overheard his parents talking about how they think it was some sort of government experiment that got out of control and that nobody would ever know the full truth.

Henry pulled the curtain back and peeked out the window. His father told him to be careful not to be seen.

Everything was empty. Blank.

A tootsie roll wrapper blew across the deserted street with the gracefulness of a leaf floating on a log.

Neighbors used to walk their dogs on the sidewalk in the afternoon here and sometimes later in the evening.

The street was cracked and covered with more craters than the moon.

Big John lived in the blue house across the street would be out cutting his grass on a day like today. Now, his lawn is covered with knee high weeds. In fact, he was the only one on the block with a nicely manicured lawn but that was mostly because he'd retired from the railroad and working on the lawn kept him busy.

That was back when things were somewhat normal. Before the fourth virus.

This one was the worst of it all. The same as the other virus they called COVID but with more bite.

Henry's grandfather banged on the door. He'd been banging on it for a week now. His parents warned him not to let him out no matter how hard he banged, pleaded and yelled and screamed.

"I just wanna sit in my rocking chair," Grandpa said. He would say it four more times.

Henry wished things were back to the way they were. Like that time, he and his dad played catch in the front yard and had talks about life. Though he felt sometimes his father got too carried away with those talks but he still liked them.

Mom would be working in the garden with her small arrangement of tulips, carnations and roses.

It was hard to believe that was the same rose bush that came from his uncle she planted when he was seven.

Now, he was thirteen. He remembered her humming to some song he never recognized as she trimmed the bush as if all was right with the world.

A few months ago, it was.

It was almost two o'clock in the afternoon. Usually, around this time, their neighbor, Chris would be out walking his dog. But he hadn't done that for months. Then Henry's dog, Scout, their white Bichon would run to the window acting like a weredog out of control barking at the other dog through the window. He barked at everybody walking down the street as if it were his. When Chris and his dog passed out of view of the window, Scout would run to the one upstairs, hop on the chair and commence the royal chewing out.

These days he just lay low on the couch and didn't move around much. He would only get up when his mother put food out for him or when they would hear an occasional gun shot.

Dogs can always sense when something bad is going to happen.

You didn't hear the shootings at first, when the virus started. Three weeks later they would hear one. Couple weeks later they would hear another. Slowly it increased to at least one a day. Now it was two or three. All within their little neighborhood.

Some sounded a little further away.

Every time a shot rang out, Scout would howl as if he knew somebody had shot themselves in the head.

Medical people said there was medicine for it. To hep prevent people from getting sick but it seemed to make everybody sick to their stomach and caused severe cramping that some women said was ten times worse than child birth.

Didn't make sense to, Henry. Taking something to prevent you from getting sick to get you sicker.

The medical people on TV really pushed the importance of getting the vaccine and when it first came out the lines would be all the way down the street and around the corner because there were only certain medical facilities that were able to administer it.

His father called it a gimmick. He said it was just the medical industries way of making even more money on drugs.

Henry supposed he was right. The medical people were pushing the vaccine pretty hard and if it hadn't been for several people getting so sick over it, nobody would have a problem taking it.

The father swore they would never take the vaccine. Never. Which is why he hadn't worked in months.

The grandfather was back to banging on the door again. So hard, Henry could see the door moving. There was no way he could get out because his father had secured the door with a 4 X 4. No way was he getting out. But grandfather sure wanted out bad.

Curse words came out of his mouth. Calling his mother and father every name in the book.

Mother felt sad for him. She wanted to let him out and was certain he wasn't going to hurt anybody, but father said there was no way, Jose. Absolutely not. Henry knew his father meant business because his father's voice so loud and deep, the way it always was when he wanted to get his point across.

Mother backed down quickly and went back to cooking dinner. Henry could tell she was having a hard time with it because it was her father. Every once in a while she snuck him food under the door which made father mad; said it would keep him strong and that was the last thing they needed right now.

This evening's dinner was fried chicken and mashed potatoes. The first time they had meat in four months since this whole thing started.

"What would happen if we did let grandpa out, Dad?" Henry asked. He knew the question was going to tick him off but he wanted to know.

"It's hard telling, son. He's all sorts of crazy right now. You saw how hard of a time he gave us trying to get him in his room. Virus done gotten in his head." He opened the cabinet and took out the gun.

"What are you doing with that?" Henry asked.

"Just never know. I have to protect you and mother."

The living room table was empty. Henry recalled the times they used to sit at the dinner table together.

Dad sat at the end because he was the boss and that was just the way it was. Once Henry tried sitting at dad's seat but his father made him get up. He said children never sit at the end of table. They are to always sit on the side.

Mother sat at the other end because she was the queen.

Grandfather sat at the side and Henry sat across from him. They laughed and made jokes and grandpa always farted at the table earning himself one of those mother looks she always gave him whenever he was up to mischief.

His father was right though. With grandpa's mind it was hard to tell what he would do. Dad said his mind wasn't right and in a very bad place. He's so crazy he would probably kill us.

Henry had a hard time believing that because grandfather wouldn't hurt a flea. Except for the way he was punching his father.

That must've been why grandpa sat at in his chair staring at the TV when it wasn't turned on. Henry would ask him what he was watching and grandpa placed his finger over his lips and shooshed him telling him he was watching his show.

Henry always wondered what his grandpa was actually watching in his mind. Every once in a while grandpa would jerk as if something startled him. Grandpa was in the Korean War, so he figured it could've had something to do with that.

Henry wished his grandfather had a lot of photos. It sure would've been nice to match the faces with grandpa's photos.

Scout was at the window barking. Henry looked and saw it was Big John standing in the middle of the street.

He had a gun in his hand.

He screamed something in some sort of language that Henry had no idea what it was, neither did anyone else.

He was shirtless and didn't have his shoes on.

Henry watched as he put the gun to his head. Henry tried to scream in hopes of interrupting it all but Big John pulled the trigger splattering his brains all over the street and his large body hit the street with a loud thud.

Something must've happened because Mrs. Riley, the poet in the neighborhood, came out waving a gun.

"Where are all these people getting these guns?" Henry asked. He never liked guns and because he never fired one he was afraid of them.

"Some people keep them for protection," His father said.

Henry nodded. "Like that time Mrs. Riley was robbed."

"Exactly."

Then out came Nathan Thompson, a man in his seventies which Henry thought was older than his grandpa but he really wasn't. All the years of drinking and smoking was hard on his body.

He pulled the trigger on himself as well.

To top it all off, Gloria Stevenson, Henry had no idea what she did except sit around all day and watch TV, came out screaming how she couldn't take it anymore and pulled the trigger.

His father told him that's what happens when people find out they're sick. Instead of trying to ride through it and hope for the best some can't handle it and just go ahead and off themselves.

"Why would somebody kill themselves over getting sick?" Henry asked. At his age he had a hard time understanding it all.

"Some just can't handle the idea," father said. "They think they'll be better off."

"Dead?"

"Yep."

"What about the medicine?"

"For some it worked for some not so much. They're really not sure. They just think you have a better chance if you take it anyway."

"Sure is confusing."

His father patted Henry's shoulder. "Tough times for sure. That's why we're just going to ride it out."

"Are we ever going to let grandpa out?"

"Why sure. Once this all clears and we know everything is ok and he's doing much better I'm sure it'll be okay."

Henry didn't know if he could handle the health department shooting grandpa. His father told him that they just have to be careful and act like nobody is here because the authorities from the health department were going to be here soon.

His father wanted to make sure they were ready in case they decide to bust down the door.

Henry didn't like the sound or looks of any of this. He'd never saw his mother and father this way before and it was scaring him.

Mother made her rounds and took temperatures. When she finished, she was always the last one to take it because mothers always take care of others before themselves, her and father looked at each other and Henry just saw her nod. Then they would smile at each other. So, Henry figured everything was OK.

Grandpa was back to having his fits again followed by his usual cursing out mother and father and saying how if he ever gets out of here they're...."

Grandpa's burst of behavior drew some concern for Henry. "What does he mean by that, Dad?"

His father bit his lower lip and shook his head. "Nothing. He's just acting up."

"He's not going to hurt us is he?"

"No, of course not."

"Sure seems like he's pretty pissed at this whole thing."

His use of the word piss caused a raise in his mother's eyebrow. "Watch your language."

"I didn't say anything bad. Just piss. Dad says it all the time."

She gave dad one of those see what I told you looks. "Still doesn't sound nice."

"I'm huuuuuungry. Feeeeeeeed me," Grandpa yelled.

Mom and dad looked at each other. Henry always found it interesting how his mother and father could communicate just by looking at each other without saying a word. It's like they were in each other's minds.

He sure wished he knew what they were talking about.

When Henry heard the sirens and saw the flashing lights his heart beat fast and he broke out in a sweat as he thought the Health Department was on their way.

"Naa." his dad said. "They'd be more secretive about it."

Henry exhaled a sigh of relief as they pulled up in front of Big John's house. Four men wearing white coveralls and masks picked up Big John and tossed him in the ambulance.

"Poor Big John. If only he would've stuck it out a little longer" his father said.

Then Henry got to thinking. "What about us, Dad? You don't think that's going to happen to us, do you?"

"No. We'll be okay. As long as we have each other we'll be okay."

Mom came running in from the kitchen telling dad and Henry it was time to get in their hiding spots.

The time has come.

She looked at dad and dad looked at her as they communicated about what they were going to do.

Dad nodded and said, "It's time."

Mom opened the trap door in the floor while his father did a quick walk through around the house making sure everything was locked up tight.

Henry wasn't sure how this was all going to go down.

Were they going to come busting down the door?

Toss a smoke grenade through the window?

He didn't know. All he knew was that he hoped they lived through this. He trusted his parents because they seemed to know what they were doing but it still didn't keep him from not being afraid.

Henry went through the trap door which lead under the house. His father made it just in time before the knock came at the door.

"Shhhhh." His father said.

They knocked four times.

Waited about a minute.

It was dirty under the house and filled with cobwebs. Henry's nose tickled as he wiped the dust away from his mouth. The two inches thick pea gravel under the house was damp giving off the mildew smell.

Knocked again.

Henry wondered what would happen if they heard grandpa. His father said they wouldn't because he boarded up his windows so there was no way. Even if they did come in they would get grandpa and not them.

A half hour later his father said that he thought they were gone and it should be safe to go on out. He instructed Henry to stay away from the windows for a while. The people from the Health Department were known to lurk around.

Grandpa must've finished his nap and started his screaming and yelling again.

Dad slammed his fist on the table. Henry figured probably because it was such a close call. "If that man doesn't shut up, I'm going to shoot him myself."

His father would too. Henry didn't think that his father cared for grandpa all that much. The way his father would scowl every time grandpa walked across the kitchen floor making that slip sliding sound with his slippers. 'Pick up your feet and walk,' he'd say.

To his father's defense Henry couldn't blame his father for disliking grandpa. Grandpa was always telling his dad how he should do this and do that and do things this way and not that. So, he could understand.

The banging from grandpa's door became louder and louder as he banged harder and harder. Grandpa was like a wild animal trapped in a cage.

Henry didn't know how it happened but there was a loudest bang he'd ever heard and all of a sudden grandpa's door flew off the hinges.

Henry's father ran toward the door with a shotgun in hand as if he were going to shoot grandpa.

Then Henry's mother came running in crying and waving her arms begging his father not to shoot him.

Henry didn't know why his father would shoot grandpa or even if he really would.

And why are his parents worried that bad. All they had to do was wear masks around grandpa and let him stay out for a little while but his father said the virus doesn't work that way.

One thing Henry was for certain was that grandpa sure wasn't happy.

Grandpa was pissed. And Henry didn't care if his mother got mad about him saying it this time. He'd never saw his grandfather so angry.

Grandpa charged out of the room with a knife which he must've had stashed away which Henry found odd because his father said he cleared the room out pretty good. But grandpa must've had it hidden for those just in case purposes.

Henry stood in the hallway as he watched grandpa plunge the knife in his father's stomach and grabbed the shotgun. Even at grandpa's age and the experience he had in the war, his father was still no match against grandpa's skills.

He pointed the gun at his mother. "I told you I'd get out of here. I told you." His grandpa said. He must've said it about five times.

"I'm sorry, Dad," his mother said. "Please. Please don't do this."

"I have to." He said. "You guys are the sickies."

"What?" Henry said. "Moooom."

"Please, Dad. No."

Henry saw a look in grandpa's eyes that he'd never saw before. It was a look of fear, sadness and anger all wrapped up in one. "I'm sooooo sorry. I have to do this before your family contaminates the area.

"I told you we were getting better. We're going to get better."

Grandpa shook his head. "Nooo. I'm afraid not. Look at Henry's hands."

Henry looked at his hands and saw small red bumps on his fingers. "Moooom. Mooooom."

Grandpa looked at Henry and his mother. "I'm sorry. But it's too late. You're all sick and all sickies must die."

SMELL OF A BABY

The baby screamed like a lobster as Clyde dropped the little feller in the pot of boiling water.

"Looky lookey here lil' fella. It's gonna be okay in a few minutes."

"How long does it take to cook the lil bastard?" Herbert asked.

Clyde and Herbert were brothers. They lived in a farm house down in the hills of Kentucky.

They ate babies.

And they needed more babies because their supply was running low and with winter coming and as of right now, they were short.

"God will provide," Clyde said. "God always provides. Just like mama said. Should be bout five minutes." He held the lid down with his arm as the baby's legs kicked out of the pot and almost flopped out. "That was a close call."

They'd be scratching at the pot and banging their head against it. Clyde couldn't blame them. He would kick and fight if someone tossed him in a pot of boiling water too.

"Almost ruined him."

"Yeah, but I didn't and that's what counts."

The baby screamed and screamed. It was music to his ears. "Usually stop screaming in three minutes and cooks fully in ten. Depending on how big and fat they are. They didn't like to get babies with too much fat. Too much fat makes them too greasy.

Clyde breathed in the aroma. "Nothing like fresh baby boiling in the evening."

"Amen to that. Too bad mom ain't round anymore to see this."

"The bestest tasting baby ever."

As it should be. They got the baby from one of the finest of homes. A home where the baby had his own crib, his own room and all the stuffed giraffe and elephants he could play with.

Cause, a happy baby is a good tastin' baby.

The house they got the baby from was a two story house with a nicely manicured lawn. After doing a little background check they discovered baby's father was a doctor.

Even better.

Cause a healthy baby is a awesome tastin baby.

The mother was young and breast feeding which meant he was getting all the good stuff which was good for his skin and promotes healthy bones.

Cause a well-fed baby is a sweet savory tastin' baby.

Clyde lifted the lid and stirred the pot with mama's wooden spoon which she called her special baby spoon. She said the wood holds all the flavors of all the others babies and make each one its own very special treat. Kind of like a nicely cured smoker.

This family had all the money in the world. As they went through their cupboards late one night just before big snatching their pantry was full of nothing but name brand baby food. Nothing but the best of the best.

And the milk? Ohhhhh, my God. 2% all the way. They tried a baby once that was fed nothing but that crappy powdery formula shit because the baby's bitch didn't have big enough tits to feed which at the time they didn't think was too bad until they tasted the lil' critter and had to throw him in the dumpster in the alley because his meat was disgusting.

This family knew what was up and knew how to take care of a baby.

His diapers were changed regularly. He could tell because most of the time there was a rash on the baby's ass.

No rashes for this lil' feller.

Nothing but baby powder.

While the parents were sleeping they snuck into the baby's room. Clyde covered the baby's mouth with a rag coated with chloroform to put him asleep. If The baby saw their faces he would surely scream and he wanted to leave all the healthy screams for the boiling pot.

He flopped the baby on his back, unbuttoned the onesie and lifted it over the baby's head.

Herbert squeezed the baby's stomach and along his ribcage as if he were picking out a healthy slab of prime rib

Hmmm. Prime baby ribs sounded good right about now. He couldn't control the saliva in his mouth

"She'd be proud of us for carrying on the tradition."

"Amen to that."

Clyde told Herbert to go check on the other babies in the basement while he watched this one.

Last time he left the kitchen he over cooked the baby and all the meat fell off the bone.

They were screaming loud this evening. Probably because nobody fed them.

It was never a good idea to feed the babies before cooking because it makes all the shit and piss come out and makes the place stink. Not to mention it makes the meat stink and tastes like shit and piss. For the best cooking, it was wise to not to feed the babies two days at least until they stop shitting and pissing. Once the diaper checks clear for a full day it's usually okay.

"Ahhhh, man, Herbert said. "You told me I could cook the baby this time. You know how I like to hear them scream when they're boiling."

"Not much to hear now. This puppy is done screaming and scratching"

"Shit, I always miss the good stuff."

"Just settle down big guy. There's more where this came from." He slapped a roach that was crawling across the counter. "Damn things. Can't stand those bastards."

There was something that smelled fresh about this particular baby. It smelled like Johnson and Johnson baby oil and powder.

Sweet yet salty.

The baby was clean. It was clean when they snagged him and it was even cleaner after he washed him in the tub and tore off his toe and finger nails. Toes and fingernails don't digest well in the stomach. This was a lesson they learned the hard way that time when Clyde had to rush to the doctor because he swallowed a couple baby and toes nails while eating their fingers and the nails poked into his intestines and damn near poke a hole in it almost causing him all sorts of problems.

He started sweating and puking and felt something jabbing at him.

The doctor shoved a camera up his ass and had a look around and told him when he came too that he needed to stop eating his nails.

So now he makes sure to pluck them off.

"This baby smells goooooooooood," Clyde said as he barely lifted the lid letting the steam roll out rewarding his nostrils with the sweet aroma. "You'd be soooooo proud, mama," he said looking at the family picture on the wall of her holding a hatchet in one hand and a baby's head in the other.

Herbert came back up from checking on the others and said everything was all fine. All locked up nice and tight in their cages.

Some of their fingers were scraped and scratched up due to them scratching at the cages. This was because they were mostly so hungry. That was okay. That was all about to change soon.

Herbert grabbed the claws and lifted the baby from the pot as if he were lifting a turkey out of the fryer.

The baby's skin was nicely charred and blistery.

"Looks good, ha?" Clyde asked.

"Looks real good," Herbert said. He chuckled. His chuckle was more like a deep guttural growl.

Clyde grabbed the scraper. "Lets get this fella all cleaned up.

They found it better to scrape off the blisters with a paint scraper with a razor blade. Got down deep in base of the blisters and scabs and scraped them off nicely.

Clyde maneuvered the baby on the counter and started scraping the skin off being careful not to scrape down to deep and tear into the meat.

The blade sunk into the top layer of the flesh, shaving off each two to three inches layer at a time. Just like shaving off the layers of meat for a gyro.

The skin smelled sweet, almost like hickory.

Knock at the door. Clyde and Herbert looked at each other.

"You expecting company for dinner?" Herbert asked.

"No. I was bout to ask you the same thing."

They knocked again.

Nobody came to visit them since mama died.

Clyde pulled the curtain away from the window. "Well now. Would you looky here."

"Who is it?"

"Some dude. Looks lost."

Clyde opened the door and there stood a man that looked nervous and looked relieved to see Clyde.

"Sir, I hate to bother you but my wife is pregnant and we are on our way to the hospital when our car broke down a mile back on the road and I saw your house and was hoping maybe you could give us a ride to the hospital." The man pulled his wallet out. "I'd be willing to pay for the gas and your troubles."

Clyde's first thought was, by the sound of his accent it was obvious they were from New York or Jersey or somewhere on the east coast. Definitely not from down here.

Clyde licked his lips. The guy was wearing a light blue Polo shirt, tan dress slacks and though Clyde didn't know what kind of shoes he was wearing but figured by the way the dude was carrying himself they were nothing less than name brand. His heart beat quickened with excitement. "Sure, we can. Wouldn't be any trouble at all. Just let me get my keys."

"Thank you, guys, so much. We really appreciate it."

"You're way off the main road for going to the hospital though."

"I was stupid and didn't think. I shouldn't have listened to my GPS. Silly me. Nerves, I guess. I really do appreciate it."

Clyde smiled a toothless smile. "You know what they say. Nothing like good ole southern hospitality."

"God will provide. He always provides."

Clyde smiled a toothless smile. "Her sure does."

SURF N' TURF

Ryder spilt coffee on himself as the ship took a heavy starboard roll and caused him to lose his balance. This was why sailors walk around with only a half cup of coffee. He cursed a few words toward the sea which had been exceptionally rough for the last couple of days.

The Chief Boats told Ryder to get a boat crew ready because the captain wanted them to go out and check on their sister ship the USS Jarret. He felt something was seriously wrong because their communications dropped instantly and the last thing the bridge heard over the radio was a lot of gurgles and screaming for help.

It was 0200 and all Ryder wanted to do was enjoy a cup of coffee before hitting the rack. He and a couple deck hands had been up all night greasing up the wire ropes for the yard and stay rigs and he was dead tired.

The chief told him he only needed to take an engineman and the boat safety officer which was LT. Hose.

LT. Hose was a large black man, and his voice was loud. Ryder and Lt. did not get along.

He cringed at the thought of the LT. coming along. The man was just too much into abiding by policies at the expense of common sense.

Ryder shrugged it off. Whatever. He was just going to have to deal with it. Hose was supposed to be leaving the ship soon to go to another station. That couldn't happened fast enough.

Ryder met the chief up on deck by the boat. The chief explained that the captain wanted to board the ship and report what they saw.

Ryder couldn't see the ship. The fog was so thick he couldn't even see his hand in front of his face.

He couldn't believe the captain was sending them out there. This was a suicide mission. "You know, Chief. We can't see where we're going out there?"

"I know. But trust me, she's bearing about just over six hundred yards."

"And the captain thinks she's disappeared?"

"We don't know. We haven't heard from her since "

"And you want to send me and my crew out there?"

"She's on our radar and the captain is certain she's out there."

Ryder thought it would be better and much safter, but let's not go overboard with the safety, he was being sarcastic but this felt like something that could wait till morning at sunrise and once the fog burns off.

The forward lookout reported hearing a loud splash and something sounded like it was crashing.

This was great. To top it off the Chief said that the captain told him that Ryder was indeed the man for the job.

This was typical. It had been that way for Ryder's entire career. Twelve years now sailing as a boatswain mate, and he was thinking that it was soon time to hang up the marlinspike.

The chief padded Ryder on the shoulder. "You can do it, Boats. I know it sucks but you really are the man for this job. I don't have anyone else that can drive a boat in these seas as well as you.

The swells were at least twenty feet and it was raining and it was extremely foggy.

Yeah, it was the perfect night to take a boat ride.

The Chief was going to owe him big time for this one once they get in port. They chatted about it and made a few jokes and Ryder told him if he comes back he's going to have to buy him all the whiskey and rum he could drink for an entire week. Then he was going to add to the reward a nice prime rib dinner at the Wagon Wheel.

The engineman was Lawless. As far as Ryder was concerned Lawless was the finest engineman in the Navy. He had got him out of several jams in the past so Ryder was glad to see Lawless was coming along. At least that's what he thought. Lawless opened the hood and gave the engine a good look over and told Ryder she was good to go and went below.

"What, no boat ride for you tonight?" Ryder asked chuckling.

"I'm on engine room watch right now. Lester is coming along for this evening's activities."

They were still waiting on the LT.

"Did somebody wake him up?" Ryder asked.

"Ridge, the boatswain mat of the watch did." The chief said. "He seemed to enjoy every minute of it too. You know how, Ridge loves irritating the Lt."

Ryder had to admit. Everybody loved irritating the LT. Any time an enlisted is awarded the opportunity to screw with an academy officer they take that ball and run with it.

Once everyone arrived and boarded the boat, Ryder had the engineman bring in the sea painter. The report was the ship was bearing 800 yards to their port side.

Shouldn't be able to miss it.

The fog was thick making visibility damn near impossible. He thought it was pretty stupid to be sent out on a day like this and even dumber on his part for even going out there looking for a ship that seemed to be dead in the water.

At this point it could be anything like a fishing boat that lost its auxiliary. Be even more comical, he thought, if it was one of those fancy cruise ships.

Rich folks think they're actually going to sea on one of those party boats.

Perhaps they should try checking on board the Jammin' Johnny for a six-month west pack. See how much they like going to sea then.

"Ever been out in seas like this, Boats?" The first LT. asked.

"Nope."

"Nope?" A hint of nervous in his tone. "What do you mean, no?"

"I mean I have not. But don't you worry, we'll be okay."

"Do you know where you're going?"

"Pretty much. Only from what the chief told me."

"Which course do we need to take?"

Already the LT. was on his last nerve by asking so many questions. Ryder pointed. "The course is that way."

Ryder and the engineman laughed.

"This isn't funny, Boats. You have to know where you're going."

"Got a good idea, sir. You just sit back and relax. Let the men do the work." The LT. was going to hate him even more for that comment.

The swell in front of them looked like a rolling mountain as Ryder throttled up and proceeded up the swell at a 45-degree angle. Once the boat reached the crest he throttled down. "Hang on."

The boat came down with a crash. Whitewater showered them. "That went well," Ryder said.

"Boats, that was a pretty rough ride," the Lt. said. "I think I have to question your boatswain mate abilities."

"Can't exactly help it, Sir. Considering we're in twenty-foot swells and in a lifeboat, I'd say we're doing pretty damn good if you ask me."

That's the difference between an academy officer and one who has worked his way up through the ranks. Ryder thought.

Lester agreed.

The boat climbed slowly up the swells reminding Ryder of a rollercoaster preparing for its trip down. Even though he had been doing this for twelve years now a trip such as this still gave him butterflies in his stomach. Ryder felt the LT holding onto his belt loop and often times grabbing him around his waist like some hot chick on the back of a motor cycle.

The Lt. was scared and soon he was certain he wasn't going to be feeling well. They had only been out there for a few minutes, but it seemed like forever. Which was comical because a sick Lt. equates to a happy crew.

Lester pointed from the bow. "Boats. What is that jumping in the water?"

To Ryder they looked like fish but why would fish be jumping around like that in the middle of the Pacific?

It looked like a school of them.

"Not sure."

At first, he thought it was just the white caps blowing from the winds but the closer they got it really did look like a school of fish.

Lt. moved as something jumped in the boat and bit his ankle. "What is this thing?"

Lt. shook his leg trying to get it off. It looked like part fish and part crab. It had sharp crab like claws but much bigger. It had the body of a crab but the tail of a fish.

"Looks like part fish and part crab," Lester said.

"Well, don't just look at it you morons! Get if off."

Ryder and Lester looked at each other with the expressions of, he sure has a set of balls to talk to us like that considering the situation he's in.

Ryder made sure he continued driving the boat and Lester grinned and glanced away.

Ryder and Lester had never saw anything like that but it sure was funny.

"Boats. Get it off." Lt. screamed as he shook his leg.

The creature ripped the Lt's pant leg as if they were a pair of scissors cutting through cloth and tore a large hole.

Claws tearing into his skin. Blood trickled between his leg and claw. Ryder could see the claw ripping off large chunks of flesh. Then, with its other claw, a much bigger claw, Ryder and Lester heard a loud snap like a small tree branch breaking as the claw severed the Lt's foot off in what seemed like one simple snap.

All of a sudden this wasn't funny anymore.

The Lt screamed with all his might as Lester stabbed the creature in its shell body with the boat hook.

Lester quickly removed his belt and used it as a tourniquet on the Lt's leg.

The meanest thought went through Ryder's mind, but he didn't feel bad about it at all. Sure, couldn't have happened to a nicer guy. Soon the Lt. was going to be discharged out of the Navy due to the hazardous situation and all he did was stand here and get in the way. Ryder and Lester were not going to get any awards for the work they've been doing but the Lt. most certainly will.

Once Lester got the Lt. taken care of he held the crab creature up. "Never quite seen anything like this. Have you, Boats?"

"Nope. Hang on. We're going up another swell."

As Ryder drove the boat up the swell and throttled down as they were on their way down they saw the creatures skimming the surface. It was a whole school of them.

"Boats. Dead ahead." Lester pointed.

What was in front of them wasn't a ship at all. They didn't know what it was at first but as Ryder got the boat closer, he changed his path to avoid hitting it and almost suddenly it was as if they had driven into a raunchy vapor cloud that reminded him of the time he found his grandmother on the floor. She had been dead for three days. Maggots ate her eyes and were chowing down on her open bed sores and all that coupled with the puss, feces and ammonia created a stretch he can still smell to this day.

The thing was floating and moving with the swells. Looking up at the thing was like looking up at a New York building. Ryder pulled the boat alongside the object and that was when they saw it.

A whale.

A huge whale. Definitely, the largest anybody had ever seen or even knew existed for that matter. Strange things have been known to happen at sea.

It was larger than an aircraft carrier.

"You think those crabs did this?" Lester asked.

"Looks like."

Ryder noticed the crabs were crawling all over the whale and backed the boat away.

Another one jumped in the boat. Clicking its claws in the air as if it were searching for anything to tear into.

SNIP…. SNIP…. SNIP….

"Don't get too close to that thing," Ryder said.

The claw waving frantically out of control in desperation.

"Keep that thing away from me," the Lt. said as he now lay in the back of the boat where he thought it was safe. The Lt. tried swatting it away, yelling at it for it to move on to something else.

The claw cut through the Lt's arm severing it at the elbow.

Blood spurted out from the stub spraying all over the boat as the Lt screamed in panic.

The other part of his arm flopped around like a fish, fingers spasming as the nerves in his arm figured out something was not right.

Ryder was busy steadying the boat and for the first time, no matter how much he hated him, he was actually feeling sorry for him.

Lester jammed the tip of the boat hook into the back of the creature. Somehow it managed to reach its large claw back and cut the wooden handle of the boat hook and released itself back into the water.

The crabby creatures were all around them. Ryder noticed they were all heading straight for the whale.

Their claws tearing off large chunks of the whale's flesh, leaving large gaps in the whale's side everywhere they chomped. Gaps large enough to create caves for them as he saw some of them climbing inside.

Another crab jumped inside the boat toward Lester but fortunately he saw it coming and rammed the splintered part of the boat hook that was now more like a spear into the crab.

The crabs surrounded them. At first Ryder thought they were heading for the boat but he realized they were in the path of the crabs as they appeared to be more interested in the whale.

They were sitting ducks in the crab's wake.

Ryder pulled the boat away and stood off to give himself a minute to think about what they were going to do.

"You think they're living in there inside that whale?" Lester asked.

"It's possible. From the looks of it I'd say so."

It also looked like the whale had been dead for a while. Ryder never smelled a dead body but he had heard nothing smelled worse but if he had to guess, this whale had it beat. Its insides rotting away like a dead chick in an egg.

Still, Ryder found there was still something very unusual about what exactly was going on here.

Crabs living inside a whale?

Behind him there were still more coming. They watched them as they climbed all over the whale's side as if they were climbing up the side of the building and some going into their caves they had dug into the whale. They had no idea why these crabs were so drawn to this area.

This had to be the largest whale any of them have ever seen. Ryder made sure he got a picture of this on his phone. Even the crabs were huge as hundreds upon hundreds claws surfaced and clicked in unison.

"Those things get too close , shoot the bastards," Ryder said.

"I don't think they're after us. They're after that whale."

The Lt. lost so much blood he was damn near unconscious.

"How's the Lt.?" Lester asked.

"He's looking rough." Ryder didn't want to say anything out loud because he didn't want the Lt. to hear but it looked like he wasn't going to make it.

"I think our job is done here," Ryder said. "We need to get the Lt. back and get him taken care of." Even though Ryder hated the guy, still he didn't want to see him hurt.

"I think you're right. Nothing else here to see."

Ryder radioed the bridge explained what happened and what they saw and that they were heading back and that the Lt. needed medical attention.

The bridge responded back that they were still receiving a ping from the Jarrett and that they had to be out there and, Ryder was right on target.

"But I don't see the ship, "Ryder said.

*Boats. Over there." Lester pointed.

Something was protruding from the whale.

"Hold on, bridge. "I think we may be on to something."

Ryder pulled the boat around but with the way the seas were tossing the boat around made it hard to get a full picture of what it was.

The Jarrett's mast was sticking out of the top right side of the whale. The radar, though bent was still rotating.

Ryder radios. "We just found the Jarrett.

His first thought was, they needed to get close enough to cut open the whale or climb into one of the caves they dug and see if anyone was still alive.

As he pulled the boat around hundreds of crabs continued to click their way into the whale so they could feed on the crew of the Jarrett.

The only thing Ryder could really do was to take more pictures of the Jarrett's mast and the crabs.

The crabs were entering and exiting through an opening in the whale's side.

Some of them carrying severed arms and legs of the crew members. Seeing that answered their question about any chance of rescue.

An attempt to climb inside the whale would be a death sentence and as far as they could tell, there were most likely no survivors.

As much as Ryder disliked the Lt. he was glad he made it through alive. He was going to have one heck of a sea story to share with his grandkids one day.

Once Ryder made his report to the captain and showed him the photos, the captain couldn't hardly believe it. A whale that size swallows a U.S. warship. He'd seen a lot of strange things at sea but never something with such biblical proportions as this.

The Pentagon granted the captain permission to destroy the whale and sink the ship which would eliminate the crabs.

Once general quarters was set and the fire control techs ready they launched three missiles.

A mushroom cloud of flesh and debris erupted and in the mist of it all a few crabs managed to rain down with several landing on the Jammin' Johnny's deck.

The crew managed to collect around one hundred dead crabs and then some.

There was an excited crew that afternoon. With the day being Sunday and holiday routine, it was going to be one heck of a surf and turf for chow

Ryder said, "You guys do realize what those crabs have been eating?"

NIGHT CALL

Ryder was not happy how it took him so long to find this house out in the middle of nowhere in the boonies.

1:00 A:M. You've got to be kidding me. Forty-five minutes from his house didn't help.

A rural area he wasn't familiar with at night with winding roads that snaked in between rolls of trees.

He cursed both the customer and the manager. Especially the manager for not having the balls to tell them we would do this tomorrow.

If it hadn't been for the rusty mailbox at the side of the road with a large arrow pointing to a gravel road he would've missed it.

The gravel road had to be at least a mile maybe more. At first he thought he might've taken a wrong turn until he saw the house at the end. A small gravel lot was to the right. He pulled his truck in there and put it in park. Tall weeds in the front yard as tall as knees. The house was an old style Victorian looking farmhouse that one should never have to go into at night. Especially as an exterminator.

The white paint on the house was flaking off and looked like it hadn't seen a paint job in two decades. It looked that bad.

There was no pathway leading up to the house. He found that odd considering most houses have a walkway leading to the front door most house like this would have stones. Maybe it was once there but decades of growth buried it.

Large bushes engulfed the front of the house covering the front door. A wood ramp led from the front door. It was obvious an old handicapped person lived here. A call like this can go two ways. One being they are the nicest people in the world and would give him coffee and cake and greatly appreciative of him being here.

The other being they are the most inconsiderate and ungrateful people with a chip on their shoulder talking the whole time about how the world has gone to hell as they complain about how things were different back in their day.

He exhaled loudly through his nose letting out an irritated snort.

He hated being on call. Being on call sucks. Never fails he would end up with a job like this.

He grabbed his phone from the bracket on the dashboard and scrolled to the work order.

Customer's name. Margie Fleming. He bit his lower lip. Just what he suspected. That was an old person's name if he ever saw one.

This was an urgency the report said.

Sure it is. Everybody has an emergency these days.

The world has a new pandemic called lack of patience syndrome.

He thought he liked things much better during covid.

The complaint read.

Rats in the kitchen running all over the house.

Well, with a house looking like this, it was no wonder. He doubted rats were running all over the house though. She probably just said that so she could get somebody out here.

Probably has only one rat. If not, more than likely a mouse.

He had only seen rats over take an entire building once in the twenty years he's been doing this, and it was a restaurant in New York. He doubted her problem was that big here in Indiana.

Still, this call could have waited until Monday.

Seriously, the office had to call him to take care of this on a Saturday?

When a tech gets a call like this most of the time it means the customer is being insistent and plays that I'm canceling my services with you if you don't do what I say card.

He hated to have to do it but if he was going to get this done he had to get it started.

Still, so early in the morning.

On that note, it wouldn't be cool if it were a big problem either. Something that would take him all night and into the morning. Not fun.

He exhaled loudly cursing how he hated to be on call and stepped out of the truck. He grabbed the metal sprayer from the extended cab and thought about what else he may need.

Houses like this usually required a lot more than what the customer originally calls for.

So, he would probably need some roach bait. He grabbed a tube and put it in the side pocket on his right leg. Glue board. Can't have enough of those. He grabbed a handful and put them in his right back pocket.

That should do it for now.

He could barely see what was once the walkway but was overgrown with weeds. Everything else was surrounded by large shrubs. Crickets chirping in the night and with it being a full moon coupled by the sound of coyotes in the background sent a little tingle around the back of his neck.

Lately, the city was being over ran by coyotes, mostly because of all the housing developments going up.

He swatted a mosquito on his right forearm and pressed the doorbell.

At least she had the light on. A white light at that. No wonder there are so many bugs flying around her porch. He made a mental note to himself about recommending changing the bulb to a yellow light. Bugs are less attracted to yellow lights which reduces the spiders.

He pressed the doorbell.

He waited. Scratched his forehead and wiped the sweat from around his face with his shirt sleeve. He hoped this lady had air conditioning. Judging from the way things looked so far, he doubted it.

"Who is it?" A raspy voice like somebody had smoked way to many cigarettes in their day asked.

"Exterminator."

"Oh, thank God."

Yeah, this was never a good sign, he thought.

He heard a latch click and the doorknob rattle as she opened the door.

This was not what he expected.

This woman.

My God. He couldn't take his eyes off her.

She sure did not look like a Margie. He pictured a much older woman. Young women these days do not have old people names and Margie was an old fogie name.

Approximately, five foot seven, blonde and wearing a light red dress that cut off just above the knees. She was thin and had all the curves in all the right places. Her smile was warm and made him feel welcome and appreciated all at the same time. He did not know too much about perfumes to know what she was wearing but wow did she smell nice.

The first thought that swept through his mind was what kind of call was this going to be?

"I'm sorry if you think I look so surprised it that voice didn't sound like you."

She chuckled. "That's my special doorbell I got on amazon."

She looked him over from head to toe to the point it was making him feel uncomfortable. It made him wonder if this were some sort of desperate housewives' type of call. Wouldn't be the first time he had a call like this.

"I see. Pretty funny actually."

"I think so. Too many people are so uptight these days. Please. Come in." She stepped aside and opened the door wider allowing him room to step in.

The house wasn't what he expected to see either. Everything was so immaculate. The living room was the first room he could see from the doorway. Oak wood floors, so glossy he could see his reflection. Victorian style furniture. An old hutch that looked to be from the late 1800's to early 1900's sat in the corner. Inside it were various sorts of white china cups and dishes. The couch and chairs in the center of the room looked like something he'd see in a western movie.

This sort of reminded him of his father-in-law telling him how in Sicily most people keep their houses looking cruddy on the outside but inside is completely different. They keep what they have a secret.

"What a lovely house," he said.

"Thank you. It was my great grandfather's. I am the only living grandchild."

"Nice inheritance. So, it says here you are having a problem with rats?"

"Ohh, yes. Very bad. I hear them crawling around at night and they make all kinds of chewing noises. I'm afraid they're going to chew my house up."

"Where have you seen them?"

"I haven't seen any yet. I know they're there. I think they're in the basement. I won't go down there by myself though."

"I see. Too creepy ha?"

"Way creepy And just the thought of rats being down there." She shivered. "Gives me the heebie-jeebies. I need a big strong exterminator to go down and check it out." She gave his biceps a gentle squeeze. "Yes. You are strong I see."

"I work out on occasion. Not as much as I'd like to though."

"Don't we all. I'm the same way. I admire people who manage to get to the gym every day to keep their selves healthy and wealthy and perfectly fit." She pinched the left side of her stomach. "Starting to get a little chubby right here."

He thought this lady was being way too hard on herself. There was nothing fat about her. In fact, she was perfect in every way. This was one call at one in the morning he was rather enjoying. And if this led to something else, well, he wouldn't mind that either.

He was feeling more comfortable now. She was making feel good.

"You know. Before you go to the basement to check it out, I know it's very late and you must've hated that you got called out at this time of night."

"Well, late night calls is part of the job at times. It's okay."

"It's not okay. The least I can do is offer you a cup of coffee."

"Now, I might take you up on that."

She guided him toward the living room and had him sit down on the sofa. This was definitely looking more and more like one of them desperate house wives calls. Either she's divorced, widowed or her husband is some sort of silly executive that is out on a business trip and leaves this beautiful woman in the large house all by herself.

If he had a wife that looked lie this his day would go as such.

Get up. Have sex. Go to work. Come home and have sex again then eat dinner and spend the rest of the evening with her in his arms and then probably have sex again.

It is possible this could turn into something more serious. Even though she was obviously older than he was. Him being only in his late twenties and she had to be, he wasn't sure. Late fifties maybe? He wasn't sure. Really didn't matter at this point. Young and old hook up all the time.

He was drawn to the family pictures on the wall to his right. One was of an older looking grouchy looking man with a mustache that curled in loops at the edges and wearing a black suit.

He loved those kinds of pictures. So much history.

To its right was a picture of a beautiful woman that very much resembled the one in this house now if she were younger. She was wearing a white Victorian style dress.

His attention was redirected to the sound of her footsteps approaching. "That's my great great grandmother and grandfather."

"Nice pictures. You look just like her."

"I get told that a lot." She handed him the cup of coffee. He held the cup just under his nose allowing the hot steam to soothe his sinuses."

"Enjoy," she said. "Then we'll check on the basement."

He sipped the coffee as she continued telling him about the pictures of her grandparent and how they left her this house under certain conditions, and she was talking about some other things that all of a sudden he didn't know what she was talking about as he felt like he was in sort of a twilight daze.

He saw her sitting across the chair talking and it was like everything turned to slow motion.

He took another sip of the coffee thinking that maybe he had come down with something all of a sudden.

He felt the cup drop from his fingers and heard a small crash as it hit the floor. He wanted to catch it before it fell but he couldn't get his body to move.

Then all went black.

He woke gasping for air. Choking. Coughing. He took a couple deep breaths. It took a minute for his breathing to return back to normal.

His heart was racing.

He opened and closed his eyes several times allowing himself to calm down. He didn't know what happened. He remembered talking to her and drinking coffee and suddenly wasn't feeling very good.

He felt something cold on his back. Very cold.

He was naked.

What the...

He saw he was lying on a stainless-steel table. A light bulb dangled from a cord above his head.

He heard the sound of water trickling and something smelled all musty and mildew as if he were in a cave.

He looked to his right and saw the walls were rocks. large rocks. Moss and mildew covered them.

This was typical for houses built back in those days. The days when houses were built to last.

To the left there was a door arch entry made of rocks that looked like it led to other rooms in the basement.

His arms and legs were spread. He tried moving his right arm to scratch an itch on his nose but realized he couldn't move it.

What's going on?

His arms and legs were strapped to the table by leather straps.

His first thought was, this is so not good. Not good at all. He wiggled and squirmed trying his best in hopes of loosening the straps.

Oh God. What is that over there?

It was like something he'd seen several times in a horror movie.

He managed to lift his head enough and saw a glimpse in from of him that looked like a cart of tools. Wood working tools.

Is that what that is?

He tried lifting his head more to try and get a better look but the leather strap around his neck prevented him from doing so.

This is like something out of that Hostel movie.

You know, he knew he shouldn't have went on this call. If he would've just stood his ground like he wanted to this wouldn't have happened.

Was the manager involved in this? Or was this just a psycho lady?

Either way, it looked like he was screwed.

He screamed for help. He figured what would it hurt. With walls made of stones like this it wasn't likely anybody was going to hear him. But you never know.

"Heeeeeeeelp! Heeeeelp!"

His voice was raspy and his throat hurt.

He inhaled and exhaled loudly as he tried telling himself little lies like it's going to be okay. You'll get through this. Everything is going to be okay. You're a big strong exterminator.

But he knew it wasn't true. From the looks of it there was no going to get out of this.

He was going to have to wait.

He wondered how long had he been down here. How long was he out for?

Oddly enough, he felt hungry.

There was a positive to this though. If you could call it a positive. His company truck was sitting just outside her house with a GPS. Surely, the manager will be wondering why he couldn't be contacted and it will show he was here.

Whatever she was planning on doing she wasn't going to get away with it.

Unless she manages to kill him before they find him.

He tried to think of something else to prevent him from going there. Kind of a tough thing to do considering he was strapped to a table in the basement of some psycho chick's house.

He moved around trying his best to loosen the straps. The strap on his right wrist was tightening and cutting into his skin.

The way she had them strapped on, the more he moved the tighter they became.

"All the wiggling and squirming you do isn't going to help you, honey bunches," she said.

Honey bunches? She thinks we're sweethearts or something? "Why are you doing this?"

"Funny how everyone says that. Simple answer really. Let's just say you excite me."

"I excite you?" Great, he really was dealing with a psycho chick from hell. "A funny way of showing it."

"Oh I know. All men say that."

"I bet they do. You know we can make this much more comfortable for both of us."

She walked to the table and picked up the small five pound sledge. "Ohhh, I think this is just perfect. You sure are a handsome fella for an exterminator." She ran her fingers down his chest. "What nice pectoral you have my dear." She slammed the sledge on his right foot.

Ryder heard the bones in his foot go crunch, excruciating pain followed.

He gasped for air. The pain radiated up his leg and around the small of his back.

"Ohhhh, baby that felt so good."

"You're a sick bitch."

"I love it when a man talks dirty. Talk dirty to me again."

"You're not going to get away with this."

"I love it. Oh baby, make me feel dirty." She slammed the sledge down on his left. Oh, God that makes me feel good. Love that crackling of the bones "

She gave him a moment to catch his breath as he gasped for air.

His lips quivered and his body shook. "My manager is going to find me. My truck has a GPS ." He thought saying that might make her stop.

"Oh, Sweetie. I've already taken care of that." She grabbed the crosscut saw from the table and sawed into the thigh of his right leg.

The teeth of the blade cut into the skin like butter. Then it hit the bone. "Wow, this makes me feel so good.

Ryder heard her sigh, gasp and moan as if in ecstasy.

He felt something cool and wet under him. He knew it was blood and he could hear it trickling down the side of the table.

By this time he could no longer feel the pain as his body's defense mechanism kicked into overdrive. Plus it looked like there were small hoses attached to his legs and into his sides with some sort of fluid running through them. She wanted to keep him alive for as long as possible. When she wanted him to feel pain she simply adjusted the fluid.

He wanted so bad to jump up from this table and hack this woman up with her own tools.

He could only watch as she hacked through his leg and listen to her as she screamed in orgasm.

She ran her hands along her breast and wiped his blood all over her now naked body. Then she started on the other leg. This time a hatchet.

Round two, sweetie pie. "You've done things to me that no man has ever done before "

CHOP CHOP CHOP

The next day Margie was in the mood again as she always was. It seemed Margie was a nymphomaniac of the worst kind

She thought about what she was in the mood for today.

What sounded good?

She scrolled through the list of numbers on her phone.

Ahhhh. She pressed the call button.

Yes, this is Margie..... No, just Margie is fine..... Umhmmm. I have a clogged drain that needs a good cleaning out and would like to schedule a service visit.

JOHNNY HAS A GUN

The day Johnny Wilkerson shot his mother his grandmother had died. Got run over by a train no doubt.

It wasn't an accident either. His grandmother owed a lot of money to a lot of people. A lot of bad people. His mother wasn't any better.

Johnny thought they both deserved what they got.

The train ripped up grandma pretty good. Whoever she owed money to had knocked her in the head and left her body lying in the middle of the tracks. She never saw it coming.

He saw chunks of flesh and bone scattered all over the tracks. To that very day there was a little spot on the rail that had never been cleaned and the incident was long and forgotten.

Blood was splattered all over the weeds that were high as knees. It was the perfect spot. Right in the middle of the woods and no houses around for miles.

Except for Johnny. Whenever he was in the area, he would check on that spot to see if it was still there. He called it grandma's spot.

Johnny loved his grandma. She was the only one who understood him and was willing to listen to him talk about how mama was such a drunk and how bad things were when she drank.

So, after learning what happened to grandma, he went to the crappy trailer which mama always called home but was really nothing more than a place for her to drink and bang her boyfriends all night.

He could still hear her moaning and groaning as her whatever boyfriend banged the snot out of her loud enough it shook the walls.

He was fed up.

Mama always treated him like crap whenever she brought a boyfriend home. Bossing him around, cursing at him and screaming about how he needs to do his part and quit making a mess in their home and to quit leaving dishes in the sink.

She was in her room when he got home. And as he suspected the door was locked. A little motel sign, DO NOT DISTURB, hung from the door knob.

He chuckled at the silly thought. Then he saw a couple roaches crawling around on the floor by the fridge and all he kept thinking to himself was how he never asked for any of this. At thirteen he was supposed to be coming home to home cooked meals and a loving mother who was supposed to be in the kitchen making cookies and daddy was supposed to be coming home soon from work and ask him how his day at school went in which case Johnny would say shitty, I got beat up today and his daddy was supposed to teach him how to fight.

Wooosh... That was exhausting just thinking about all that.

Johnny learned real quick that life did not work out that way.

It sucks.

Nothing works like it's supposed to. He saw it with his own eyes. His mother. No wonder daddy went out for milk one night, three years ago and never came back. The least his father could've done was take him with him.

No. Left out in his rusty ole pick-up.

He remembered standing at the doorway in this very spot. "Daaaaaad. Come back. Come back daaaaaaad."

Tough shit, son. The voice inside his head said.

It made him mad just thinking about it.

He took the 9mm out from under his bed that he kept there to protect himself because there were always a lot of burglaries going on. Nobody had any money here at the trailer park but it was easy pickins' for the crackheads.

He tried the knob. The door was locked. They were too busy into each other to realize somebody was standing by the door. Even though it was locked it wasn't a good lock and with a little extra force it would open.

There she was on top of whatever that fat creature of a pig thing was just going to town in all her drunken stupor. He could tell she was so drunk she couldn't even bounce straight.

He was so pissed. He could feel his insides rumbling like a volcano about to erupt with a fiery vengeance.

His mother deserved men like this. Men that took advantage of her willingness to give up her sex for any man who would show her any interest or wine and dine her and not necessarily in that order either. Mother was real good at spreading her legs. Often the cumtwats gave her a few bucks for groceries after they sat in the chair in the living room watching TV and drink all of her beer and whiskey.

She deserved men who would slap her around like she was a rag doll and kick her around treating her like a dog.

The fat creature saw him looking and yelled. "Get your pervert of a son out of here," he yelled.

Mama stopped bouncing and turned and looked. "Go on, Johnny. Close the door. We're in the middle of something here."

He hated his mother too. Hated her for all it was worth. Instead of banging some dude that was only going to give her a few bucks and let him cum all up inside of her as if she were a blow up doll, she was supposed to be in the kitchen making him supper like all good mothers.

But that was if she was a good mother.

She wasn't a good mother.

Her eyes moved to what he was holding in his hand. She didn't say anything. The fat creature yelled and called him a bitch and that pissed Johnny off even more. He told Johnny to get the F... out and find his own bitch.

Johnny thought he was right about one thing. Mama was a bitch.

Johnny raised the gun. The first shot hit mama in the face and she fell over dead while still inside him. The fat creature tried hiding behind mama but Johnny put a couple more bullets in mama to make sure they went all the way through and got him.

His arms collapsed to his sides and his eyes stared straight at the ceiling as if he were some stroke victim that lost his mind.

He opened the door and stepped out. It was dark now and getting late. He looked around. Lights were on in some of the other trailers and some country song, he recognized as Merle Haggard was playing from a near-by trailer but nobody seemed to hear anything.

As he stood at the doorway, he could hear the soft ticking of the wooden clock his grandmother gave mama. It looked very much like a cuckoo clock without the cuckoo bird.

TICK...Tick... Tick... Tick...

Time keeps on ticking. Time keeps on moving and it didn't care there were two people dead inside.

Instead of leaving right that instant he went into the kitchen, opened the fridge and took out a beer and drank it all down.

He had drank beer before. It wasn't his first rodeo. The beer was cold and tasted good going down his throat. Fat creature wasn't man enough to drink real beer like an ale or a lager. Instead, he bought a case of Ole Milwaukee that was on sale for a couple bucks a six pack. Piss water he called it.

Real men drink real beer and real whiskey.

When he was done, he felt like drinking another. So, he did. He drank it while staring at the lifeless bodies in front of him. Mama's eyes wide open. Fat man lied face down. His naked butt sticking out from under the covers.

Neither one of them had much to say now.

The beer tasted good.

He opened another and he was feeling pretty good.

While he drank his beer, he started remembering a time when his mother smacked him across the face because he was getting smart mouthed with one of her bar room lovers.

It wasn't the smack that hurt, well, except for the little bit of sting. It was the first time she had hit him in anger and that bothered him.

It wasn't the first time for bar lover boy though. He'd punched him in the face five different times. He said that he was in charge now, since his real father left and he said he was his daddy now he had better behave himself if he knew what was good for him.

Johnny was like no way am I calling him dad.

Johnny felt he had no choice but to shoot them. If he wanted to be free, really free and live a good life they would have to die. It was that simple.

He thought pulling the trigger would be the hard part.

He was shocked. It wasn't.

Pulling the trigger was easy- peasy. Probably the easiest thing he had ever done.

Living with the look of fear he saw in their eyes. Now, that was another story.

Mama crying, begging him.

Of course, the punk boyfriend who thought he was all that learned real quick that he wasn't all that at all. That feeling of, oh what have I just done had swept over him quick, like a ghost.

There was no undoing this one. No going back

He put the gun to his head and pulled the trigger.

Don't miss out!

Visit the website below and you can sign up to receive emails whenever Christopher Ridge publishes a new book. There's no charge and no obligation.

https://books2read.com/r/B-A-RYTC-UGRKC

Did you love *Sickies*? Then you should read *Shouldn't Play with Dead Things*[1] by Christopher Ridge!

A five story collection of short dark humorous horror stories. If you like dark humor and gory, these tales may be for you.

Read more at creaturecritter.blogspot.com.

---

1. https://books2read.com/u/49ddYY

2. https://books2read.com/u/49ddYY

Also by Christopher Ridge

Hairy Scary Eight Legged Engineers
HOME INVASION
Bug Spray not Included
DateBite
Giant Steel Death Machines
The Ugly Truth About Shopping Carts
Dead End Job
Lobster Woman of Bubwater
Hatchet Hall
There's a Man on that Street
CUT'M UP TALES
Severance
The Fling
Macabrre Monthly
Strikeout
Splat
Slime
Because Google Said
Demented Tales
Captive
The Ghost Pirate
Clickety Clackers
Bumper to Bumper

The Hatch
Help Wanted
Creatures
Shouldn't Play with Dead Things
Sickies

Watch for more at creaturecritter.blogspot.com.

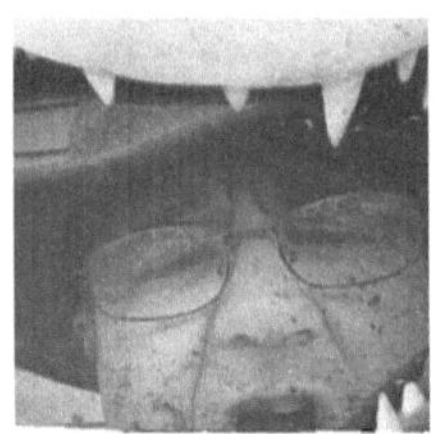

About the Author

Christopher Ridge is a creature feature horror and sci-fi writer. He enjoys B horror movies, aliens, monsters and mutant insects and such. To get an idea of what his stories and short novels are like think ATTACK OF THE KILLER TOMATOES, THEM, and IT CAME FROM OUTER SPACE. He lives in Indianapolis Indiana with his wife and two sons.

Read more at creaturecritter.blogspot.com.

www.ingramcontent.com/pod-product-compliance
Lightning Source LLC
Chambersburg PA
CBHW022112150726
47990CB00003B/1337